OH! THOSE CRAZY DOGS!

A TRIP TO THE COTTAGE WINTER AND SUMMER

BOOK NINE

CAL

ILLUSTRATED BY:
RACHAEL PLAQUET

To order additional copies of this book, contact:
Xlibris
844-714-8691
www.Xlibris.com
Orders@Xlibris.com

ISBN: Softcover 978-1-6698-5924-6
EBook 978-1-6698-5923-9

Print information available on the last page

Rev. date: 12/13/2022

OH! THOSE CRAZY DOGS!

A TRIP TO THE COTTAGE
WINTER AND SUMMER

Introduction

This is a story about 2 crazy dogs, their adventures and the mischief they get into.

They are very loving dogs, but they can't help getting into things.

Hi ! I'm Colby! I'm big and red and furry ! I love everyone but sometimes people are afraid of me because I am so big!

Hi! I'm Teddy Bear! I'm big and white and very furry! I'm not as big as Colby, but just about. Everyone thinks I'm cute and I put shows on for them.

He puts shows on for everyone, rolls on his back and kicks his legs up.

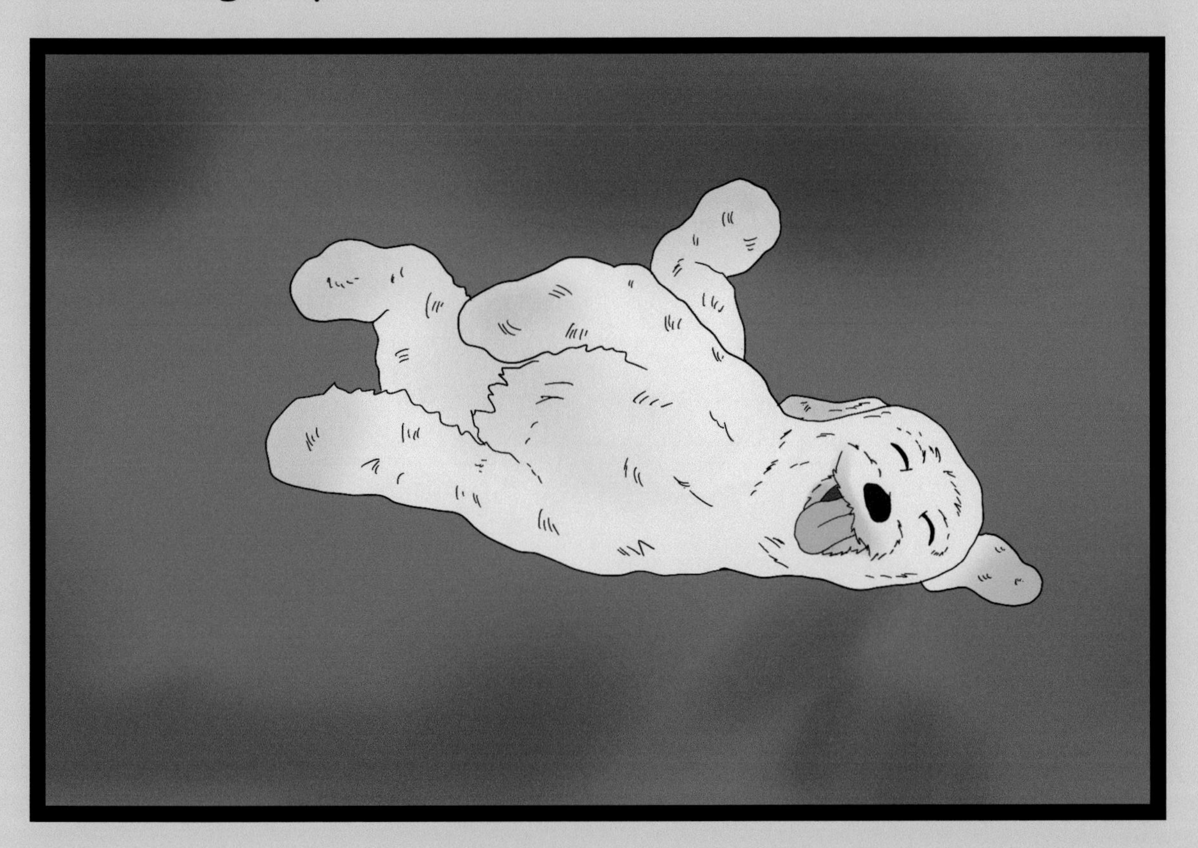

Our owners picked us out specially and brought us home to love and care for us. We love them too, very much. They give us everything and a warm loving home. We will call them Mom and Pop.

Sometimes we don't listen to them, especially me, Teddi Bear!

Our Mom and Pop love us anyway. Sometimes I get Colby in trouble. I can get him to do anything I want because he loves me too and can't say no. He protects me all the time.

The Winter Trip

"Colby, Colby I think we're going to the cottage! Mom and pop are packing up a lot of clothes and food and toys like before!"

"Yes", said Colby "I guess we are! That's great because there will be a lot of snow there!"

"Yay" said Teddi Bear, "we hardly ever get snow here so it will be a lot of fun playing in it. I remember the last time we had snow here we had a nice adventure!"

"Yes, we did. That was when Digger came home with us and stayed for awhile. It was really nice of the neighbours down the street to give Digger a good home." said Colby.

"Yes it was" agreed Teddi Bear. "I'm going to get some of my things so mom and pop don't forget them!" Teddi bear ran off leaving Colby looking puzzled. Within five minutes Teddi Bear had piled all of his favourite toys by the door. Colby laughed "Good luck with all that!" exclaimed Colby.

"Mom and pop came to the door with the suitcases and boxes. They laughed when they saw the pile of toys at the door. "Oh Teddi Bear, I've already packed your best toys and you still have some at the cottage. I don't think you'll get bored." Mom stooped down and gathered up all his toys at the door. She went to put them back in his toy box.

"Okay boys let's go!" Mom opened the door and pop was standing there with the van door open for them. They ran into the van taking their positions as usual. Teddi Bear in the middle and Colby between mom and pop.

The ride was long but they knew at the end of it they were going to have a lot of fun. Finally, they got to the cottage and pop got out to open their door to let them out. Colby and Teddi Bear ran and jumped into all the snow. Pop grabbed a shovel to clear a path to the door then he and mom unloaded the van.

Teddi Bear was running in circles and Colby was running up and down the hill. "This is great!" exclaimed Colby, "it's so cool and fluffy!" Their coats were full of snow.

"Okay boys, come on in. Time to get dried off and have your supper." Teddi Bear and Colby went into the cottage, ate and cuddled with mom and pop until they all went to bed.

The next morning mom and pop let us out to do our business (hee, hee). We ate a small breakfast and ran back outside. There was so much snow here! The wind had blown the snow into many snowdrifts and snowbanks. Teddi Bear and Colby were in their glory. They would chase each other back and forth. They would run through the deep snow drifts and poof, come out on the other side.

"Come and get me Colby!" yelled Teddi Bear and he ran off. Colby jumped up and started running after him.

"I'll get you Teddi Bear! Watch out! I'll get you!" Teddi Bear laughed and ran up the hill. He hid behind a snow drift waiting for Colby. As soon as Colby got to the top of the hill Teddi Bear jumped out at him laughing. "I got you!" yelled Colby and made a fast backward turn and ran down the hill with Teddi Bear close behind him.

Colby made a sudden stop and Teddi Bear went rolling over and over and landed in a big snow drift with a loud poof! Colby was laughing so hard that he sat down and when Teddi Bear's head came up from the snow drift he was covered in snow and laughing too! "Oh, Colby you tricked me! He ha ha ha! That was so much fun!" Teddi Bear shook off all the snow. "We should go in the cottage for now, I'm wet, hungry and tired" said Teddi Bear.

"Me too" said Colby, "let's go in.

They cuddled with their mom and pop again before they went to sleep for the night. The next morning Colby and Teddi Bear ate breakfast and went outside. It was snowing big, fat, fluffy, flakes (say that 3 times in a row!) it was really beautiful. “Hey “said Colby, “I didn’t notice that the lake was frozen yesterday. How about if we slide down that clear area with no trees?”

Wow that's a good idea!" said Teddi Bear, "let's do it !" Teddi Bear sat on his bottom and Colby gave him a good push. Away he went "whee! Oh boy" he exclaimed. Colby watched as Teddi Bear went sliding down the path onto the snow filled beach and onto the icy lake.

All of a sudden Teddi Bear started twirling around and around in a circle. Faster and faster he went. "Wow" said Teddi Bear, "how do I stop?"

"I'm coming!", yelled Colby. He took a run then sat down on his bottom. Colby went sliding down the path over the sand onto the ice on the lake.

He was aiming straight for Teddi Bear who was still twirling in circles. “Here I come” yelled Colby. Colby slid right into Teddi Bear and they both went sliding across the ice.

"Put out your foot" said Colby. Both Colby and Teddi Bear Put out their feet and skid to a stop. "Oh wow! That was so awesome!" exclaimed Teddi Bear.

Colby just shook his head. "Aren't you even dizzy?" he asked.

"Well yes, ha, ha, but it was so much fun, I can't believe it!" replied Teddi Bear.

Colby and Teddi Bear started walking back to the cottage, slipping and sliding all the way.

Mom and pop were outside on the porch watching them. "What are you two boys doing?" asked mom. In response Teddi Bear rolled over in the snow kicking his feet in the air Colby ran circles around Teddi Bear.

Mom Looked at pop and said "Oh! Those crazy dogs!"

The Summer Trip

Colby was looking out the window when Teddi Bear ran up the stairs and said, "Colby, Colby, I think we're going back to the cottage! Mom and pop are packing up all our things again! Oh boy, oh boy! It's summer now and there won't be any snow but we can still have fun!"

"Let's go downstairs and see if they're ready yet." said Colby They went down stairs and mom said, "you're just in time, let's get in the van because we're going to the cottage!"

"Yay! Let's go Colby!" said Teddi Bear.

Everyone got into the van and away they went on the long drive to the cottage. As soon as they finally arrived pop opened the side door of the van to let the dogs out. Colby and Teddi Bear jumped out of the van and ran around in the yard to burn off some energy. "Yay! We're here, we're here!" yelled Teddi Bear.

While mom and pop unloaded the van Colby and Teddi Bear ran down the stairs to the beach. Teddi Bear looked at Colby and asked "Do you think we can go into the lake now?"

"I don't know Teddi Bear. If we do, we'll be soaking wet and have to stay on the porch to dry off and it's getting late so we should go back up to the cottage." said Colby.

"Okay, let's go" said Teddi Bear.

The two dogs ran up to the cottage and mom and pop let them in. They had supper and cuddled with mom and pop before they all went to bed.

In the morning, after breakfast, everyone went down to the beach. Pop had set up all the chairs for them to sit on and Colby and Teddi Bear ran into the water, jumping the big waves

All of a sudden a big boat slowly came up to the beach where they were sitting. Mom and pop hugged the man who jumped off the boat. They talked for awhile and Colby and Teddi Bear lay on the shore.

Then mom and the man (who turned out to be her brother) got into the boat and started to slowly drive away out into the lake. Colby looked at Teddi Bear and yelled "No, you can't take my mom without me! I have to watch her!" Colby jumped into the lake and began swimming after the boat.

"Colby, Colby please come back" yelled Teddi Bear "You're going too far!" Then pop got off his chair and walked a bit into the lake

"Colby" he yelled "come back here. Come back here now!" Colby ignored them both. He was very protective over his mom and he had to get her back! Colby kept swimming after the boat but it was getting further and further away. He couldn't swim as fast as the boat.

Colby stopped swimming and looked back at the shore where pop and Teddi Bear looked very small. "Oh no" exclaimed Colby, "I really did swim too far! But my mom! Where is she? He was very upset that his mom was gone. "Oh my, I better work very hard to get back to the beach." Pop and Teddi Bear looked really worried but Colby was a good swimmer and kept paddling his four legs to get to the shore while pop and Teddi Bear watched him.

When Colby finally got back to the beach, he flopped down on mom's beach bed to catch his breath and watch for her. Teddi Bear and pop ran over to him. Pop hugged him and said "Ah Colby I was so worried about you!" Teddi Bear sat down beside Colby "And you say I'm crazy!" he said. "I think you were half way across the lake"

Colby stood up and started pacing back and forth on the beach, barking at mom to come back. He was very worried about her. "Colby, mom is okay. She will come back. Mom just went for a boat ride with her brother" said Teddi Bear, trying to calm him down, but Colby kept pacing the beach watching for mom to come back. Teddi Bear couldn't do anything to calm Colby down so he just lay on the beach and waited.

Mom wasn't gone too much longer and finally they saw the boat coming back to the beach. Colby started barking and jumping up and down. Pop said "okay boys, come here, let mom get off the boat. Pop grabbed their collars and waited while mom got off the boat.

Mom said "it's okay, let them go because they were whining and crying and jumping. Mom didn't know what had happened while she was gone. Both dogs raced to greet mom and both jumped on her at the same time. Oomph, down she went into the sand with two large doodles on top of her.

They were both jumping up and down and trying to lick mom. Mom shouted at pop. "Get these boys off me!" pop came and helped mom up.

"Oh my goodness" said mom "I wasn't gone that long!" Pop told her about Colby. "Oh, Colby you are so sweet. You don't have to worry about mom, I was having fun! How about if we all go out in our boat tomorrow?" "Yay! Said Teddi Bear and Colby and they both looked out at their boat moored out in the lake.

Mom said "come on everyone, let's go up and eat" Colby and Teddi Bear played in the front yard for the rest of the day. Teddi's favourite toy is a large squeaky chicken. He always has it with him. That afternoon mom's brother came over to chat with mom and pop. He had a dog with him. The dog was kind of like us but not quite. She was a bit shy or nervous.

Suddenly mom and pop noticed that Teddi Bear was no where to be seen. They all started looking everywhere for him. Mom's brother noticed his dog was gone too so he said she had probably just gone home.

Teddi Bear would go there so mom's brother walked over to his cottage and found both dogs. He called his dog and Teddi Bear followed her. Teddi Bear stayed close to her side. He was almost glued to her.

Mom noticed that her brother's dog had Teddi Bears chicken but her brother said he didn't think his dog would take Teddi Bear's chicken because she had her own. Mom said Teddi Bear's chicken was missing though. So her brother went back to his place with his dog and Teddi Bear glued to her side and found his dog's chicken. He threw her chicken at Teddi Bear but he didn't even acknowledge it, he wanted his own.

The man took Teddi Bear's chicken out of his dog's mouth and threw it at Teddi Bear. He caught it and ran like crazy with his chicken in his mouth. Breathless Teddi Bear said "Colby, you watch her, she steals things" and Teddi Bear went and put his beloved chicken up on the porch by mom's chair to keep it safe.

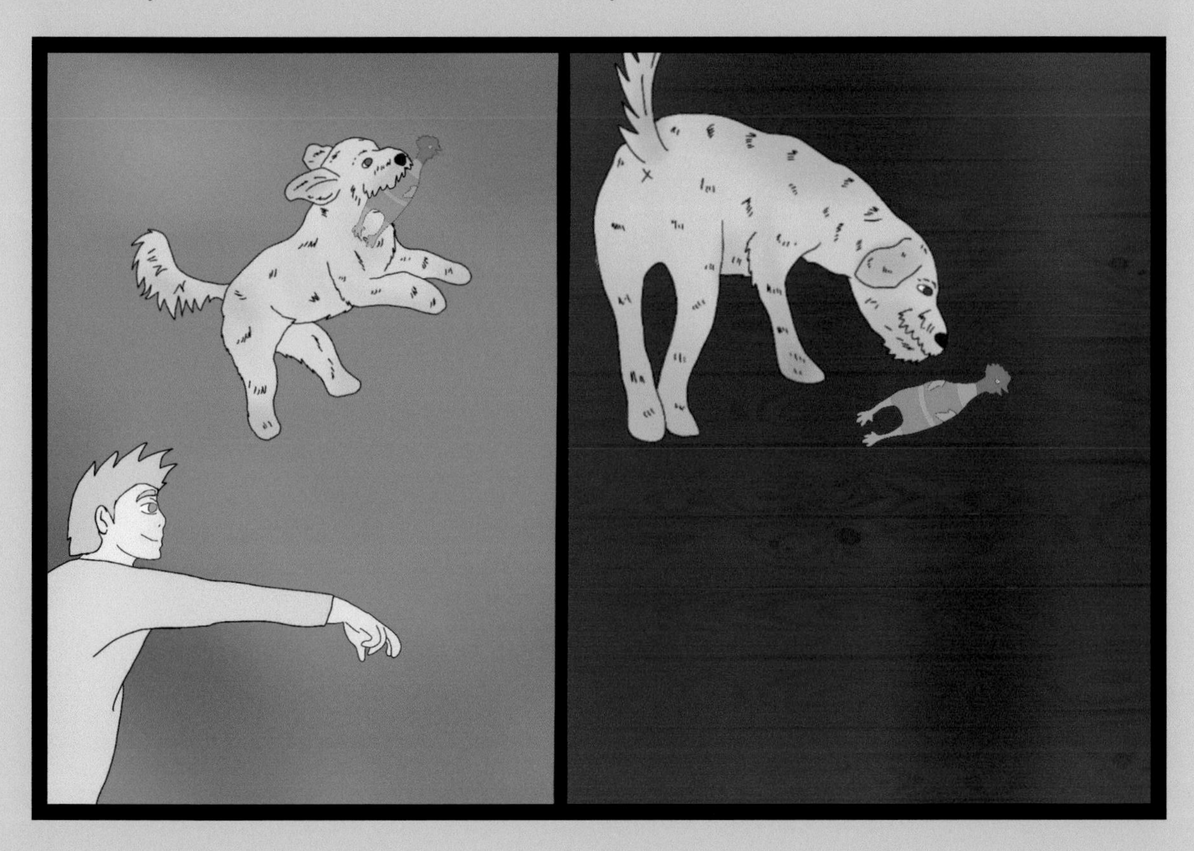

The next morning after breakfast, mom packed up a few things to bring on the boat. Colby and Teddi loved the boat, especially Colby. They swam while mom and pop walked through the water to the back of the boat.

Pop pulled the ladder down and Colby climbed up the ladder and jumped into the back of the boat. Teddi Bear climbed up the ladder next, then mom.

She got into the driver's seat and put the motor down. Teddi Bear was pacing in the boat because he didn't know where to sit. Mom held his collar and told him to sit next to her. Colby had gone right to the seats in the front of the boat and sat on those. Mom called Colby her hood ornament! Pop came in the boat and pulled up the ladder. Pop sat down across from mom, took Teddi Bear from her and off they went.

This boat went very fast. Teddi Bear said "Colby I want to sit up there with you."

"No replied Colby "you're too active and a bit nervous. You can't sit still so would probably fall into the water" They drove around the lake for awhile then started back to the cottage.

Mom was slowing down as we got closer to the shore. As the boat got closer to the beach Teddi Bear and Colby were getting excited. They were just about there when mom stopped and let Colby and Teddi Bear jump off the platform at the back of the boat. Teddi Bear said "wow, that was fun! I'll race you back to the beach Colby."

"You're on Teddi Bear" said Colby. Although Teddi Bear was fast Colby was big and powerful. The waves were up and Colby just jumped over them while Teddi Bear had to swim through them. Colby beat Teddi Bear by about a foot. "There you go I beat you!"

"I'll race you up the stairs to the cottage!" said Teddi Bear and he raced up the stairs ahead of Colby. When Teddi Bear was up the stairs he started rolling in the grass and kicking his feet up in the air. Colby came up the stairs with mom and pop.

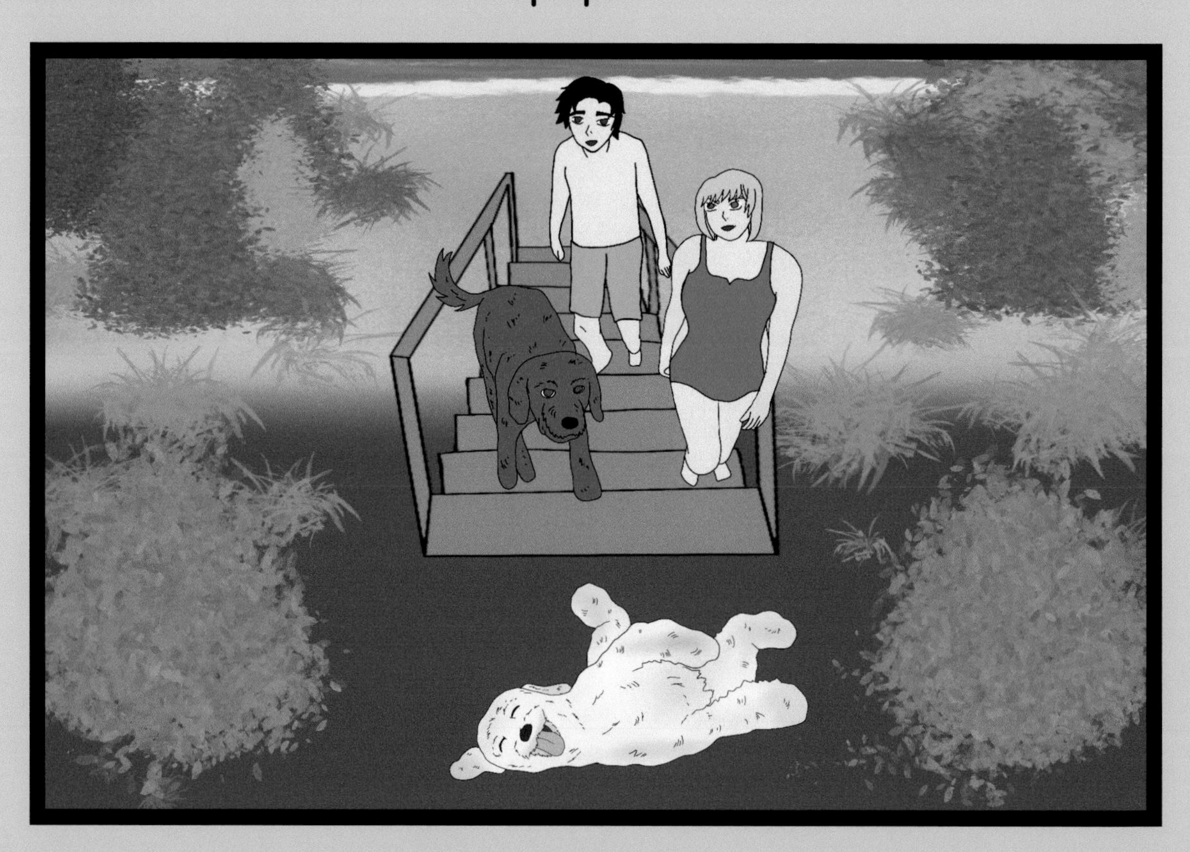

They both lay down on the porch to dry off while mom and pop went into the cottage. After supper they were all tired and sat outside for awhile looking at the lake and stars and the full moon shining on the lake. Colby and Teddi Bear were more interested in the sounds and smells all around them, but they had to stay on the porch with mom and pop. There were some interesting smells out there though! We really liked being outside.

Sometimes late at night mom would sit outside on the balcony and bring both of us with her. We liked that too. For the next few days' the weather was beautiful and we all spent the days on the beach, swimming and going boating. Mom would swim far out in the lake and Colby would follow her and try to get her to come back. He would swim around her and herd her back.

Teddi Bear would swim and catch his ball and sometimes sticks. One time Teddi Bear found a great big stick floating in the lake and brought it to shore. "Wow!" exclaimed Colby. "I think that stick is bigger than me." Colby swam with Teddi Bear back to shore.

Teddi Bear dropped the stick on the beach and began digging more deep holes in the sand, spraying it all over as usual.

When going for the boat rides Colby would always get to the boat first. He would hang on to the platform and wait for mom or pop to pull the ladder down. Up he went and ran to his spot on the front seat. Teddi Bear would climb up the ladder and sit on the floor between mom and pop. It was a lot of fun.

Mom always drove the boat and sometimes she would go over big waves and make big bumps.

When mom and pop started packing up, we were a little sad. We started running all around the yard. We weren't allowed to go on the beach or in the lake because we would get the van dirty or wet on the way home.

Then it was time to go home. We all got in the van and began the long ride home. We were happy and content.

"So now when we get home, we are going to jump in the pool!" said Teddi Bear. "Hmm" said Colby. He was tired and lay down on the floor between mom and pop. Teddi Bear, as usual, sat up in the middle seat and looked out the window watching everything. Mom looked at both dogs and shook her head with a smile on her face. When they did get home, both Colby and Teddi Bear ran and jumped into the pool.

Mom looked at pop and said “Oh! Those crazy dogs!”

Thank you for choosing this book to read. Please watch for book 10 coming out soon!

Books in the "Oh Those Crazy Dogs"
Series by author **CAL**

Book one	Colby Comes Home
Book two	Teddi Bear Comes Home
Book three	Teddi Bear's First Time at the Lake!
Book four	A New Friend in the Neighbourhood! Digger!
Book five	Teddi Bear and Colby Love Swimming in the Pool
Book six	Colby and Teddi Bear Go To The Circus
Book seven	Tyse Comes To Visit
Book eight	Winter Fun
Book nine	Fun At The Cottage - Winter and Summer
Book ten	We're Moving!

Printed in the United States
by Baker & Taylor Publisher Services